D0099908
To: ______________________
Love: ______________________

To the tremendous love that
I hold in my heart for my family
—GU

For S, always
—JB

An imprint of Bonnier Publishing USA
251 Park Avenue South, New York, NY 10010

Manufactured in China HUH 0618
First Edition 10 9 8 7 6 5 4 3 2 1
Library of Congress Cataloging-in-Publication Data
Names: Urda, Gary, author. | Bell, Jennifer (Jennifer A.), 1977- illustrator.
Title: Love you more / Gary Urda; illustrated by Jennifer A. Bell.
Description: First edition. | New York, NY: Little Bee Books, [2018]
Summary: Parents tell their child that, although they once thought they knew about love,
their child's presence in their lives has taught them what true love is. | Identifiers: LCCN 2017057015
Subjects: | CYAC: Love—Fiction. | Parent and child—Fiction. | BISAC: JUVENILE FICTION / Family /
New Baby. | JUVENILE FICTION / Family / Parents. | JUVENILE FICTION / Love & Romance.
Classification: LCC PZ7.1.U73 Lov 2018 | DDC [E]—dc23 | LC record available at https://lccn.loc.gov/2017057015
ISBN 978-1-4998-0652-6
littlebeebooks.com
bonnierpublishingusa.com

LOVE YOU MORE

by Gary Urda

illustrated by
Jennifer A. Bell

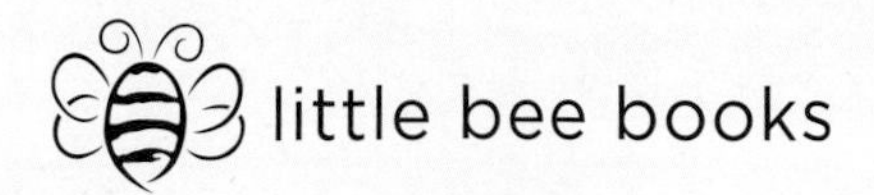

We thought we knew what true love was...

but then you came into our lives.

I love you more than all the sleepless nights...

and all the early, tired mornings.

I love you more than all the cereal on the floor...

and all the spilled milk too.

I love you more than all the raindrops falling from the sky...

and all the puddles we splashed in.

I love you more than all the blooming
springtime flowers...

and all the dandelions we made wishes on.

I love you more than all the blades of grass at the park...

and all the soccer that we played.

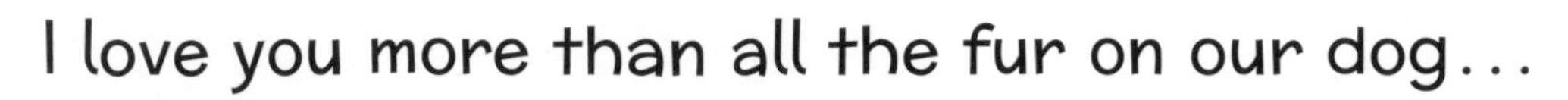

I love you more than all the fur on our dog...

and all the walks we took together.

I love you more than all the sand on the beach...

and all the waves we played in.

I love you more than all the fish in the ocean...

and all the shells we collected.

I love you more than all the branches in the trees...

and all the leaves
that fell from them.

I love you more than all the games we enjoyed together...

and all the laughs we shared.

I love you more than all the snowflakes
falling on a cold, wintry day...

and all the snowmen we made.

I love you more than all the lights twinkling on our tree...

and all the
decorations we hung.

We love you more than all the stars in the sky...

and all the miles to the moon and back.

14

We thought we knew what true love was,
and now we do... because of you.

Author's Note

Family is a very important part of my life; it always has been. I had thought the love of my life was my wife, Nicole, but after we had kids, I realized that the love a parent has for a child is a whole different kind of love.

Love You More comes out of a silly thing I sometimes did with my boys when tucking them in at night. When they said, "I love you," I would reply, "I love you more." At one point, we started adding more descriptive definitions of our love. A favorite was when one of my sons said, "I love you more than infinity" and gave me a look that said, "Top that one, Dad." I responded with, "I love you more than infinity . . . plus one."

Giving voice to the depth of our love has made us closer. This book is dedicated to the tremendous love that I hold in my heart for my family: my three sons—Tyler, Sean, and Luke—and my beloved Nicole.

14